Rules at School

Rules in the Playground

Dwayne Hicks

illustrated by
Aurora Aguilera

PowerKiDS
press

New York

Published in 2020 by The Rosen Publishing Group, Inc.
29 East 21st Street, New York, NY 10010

First Edition

Editor: Elizabeth Krajnik
Art Director: Michael Flynn
Book Design: Ricardo Córdoba
Illustrator: Aurora Aguilera

Cataloging-in-Publication Data

Names: Hicks, Dwayne, author.
Title: Rules in the playground / Dwayne Hicks.
Description: New York : PowerKids Press, [2020] | Series: Rules at school | Includes index.
Identifiers: LCCN 2018024145| ISBN 9781538344385 (library bound) | ISBN 9781538345702 (pbk.) |
  ISBN 9781538345719 (6 pack)
Subjects: LCSH: Playgrounds--Safety measures--Juvenile literature.
Classification: LCC GV423 .H53 2020 | DDC 796.06/8--dc23
LC record available at https://lccn.loc.gov/2018024145

Manufactured in the United States of America

CPSIA Compliance Information: Batch #CSPK19. For further information contact Rosen Publishing, New York, New York at 1-800-237-9932.

Contents

Hunter is in kindergarten. Today his class is going to the playground!

4

"Remember the rules of the playground," Mr. Wu says.

"When you hear the whistle,
it's time to go inside."

Hunter wants to play foursquare.

He waits his turn.

It's a new game.
It's Hunter's turn to play.

Hunter sees James climbing the fence.

"You're not supposed to climb the fence, James. It's not safe."

Hunter sees a cup on the ground.

Hunter puts the cup where it belongs.
There's no littering on the playground.

Hunter waits in line for the slide.

Two boys are pushing each other.

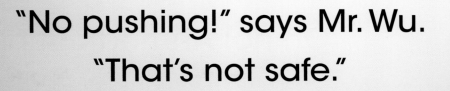

"No pushing!" says Mr. Wu.
"That's not safe."

Oh no! Ahmed cut his knee!

Hunter gets Mr. Wu right away.

Hunter sees that Stacy
is sitting alone.

Hunter plays a game with Stacy.

Mr. Wu blows his whistle.
"Time to clean up!" he says.

20

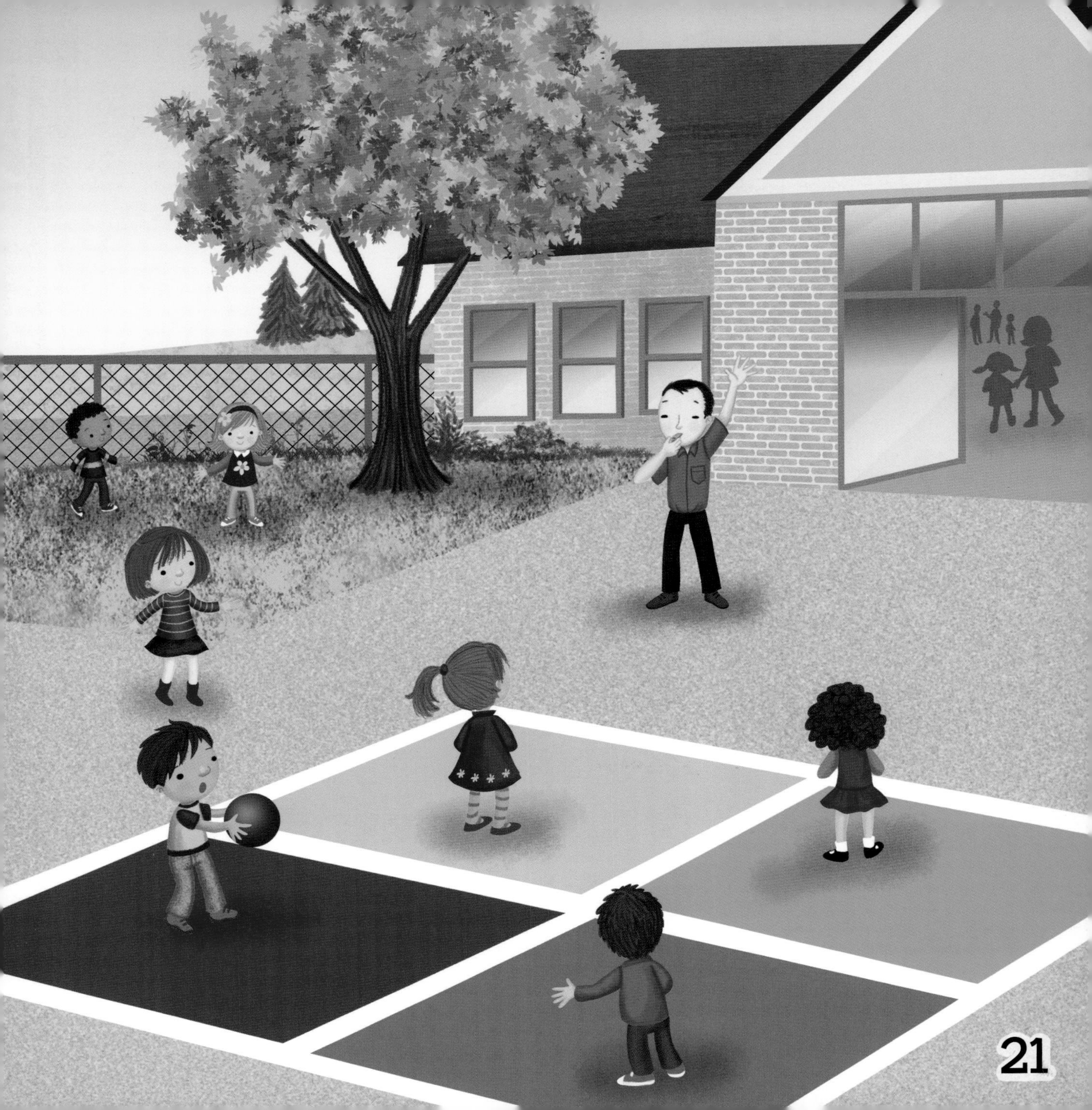

Hunter and Stacy clean up the game.

Everyone lines up to go inside.
Hunter knows the rules
of the playground.

Words to Know

fence

slide

whistle

Index

C
cup, 12, 13

F
foursquare, 8

G
game, 9, 19, 22

K
knee, 16